I knew my Mum was fast, as she was Harriet Powerful one of the fastest female runners in the world. She was known for being a famous athlete.

My Dad Nelson Powerful, played for one of the top Premier League Football teams and he was very strong. I thought all Dads had his strength, I was wrong.

My older sister Cleo, was top of all her classes,she was super brainy, she enjoyed learning about space and the universe.

$x = \frac{-b \pm \sqrt{b^2 - 4ac}}{2a}$
1st

My family won every event at sports day and Cleo won first place at the science fair, every year, even then I did not think it was because we had special powers

1
2
3

**My twin brother Martin,loved to daydream and most of his dreams came true,I on the other hand,always thought I could hear other peoples thoughts, as I could tell them exactly what they were thinking, before they said it out loud.**

CHECK MATE
DANGER AHEAD
I KNOW YOUR EVERY MOVE
CHECK MATE

It was strange how we were good at everything, however that Sunday, I would find out why.

Martin was winning the basketball game, when Mum asked us to come inside.

Cleo and Dad were sitting in the front room, waiting for Martin and I. Mum told us to sit down, then she explained to us how our 8th birthday tomorrow,was going to be a very special one.

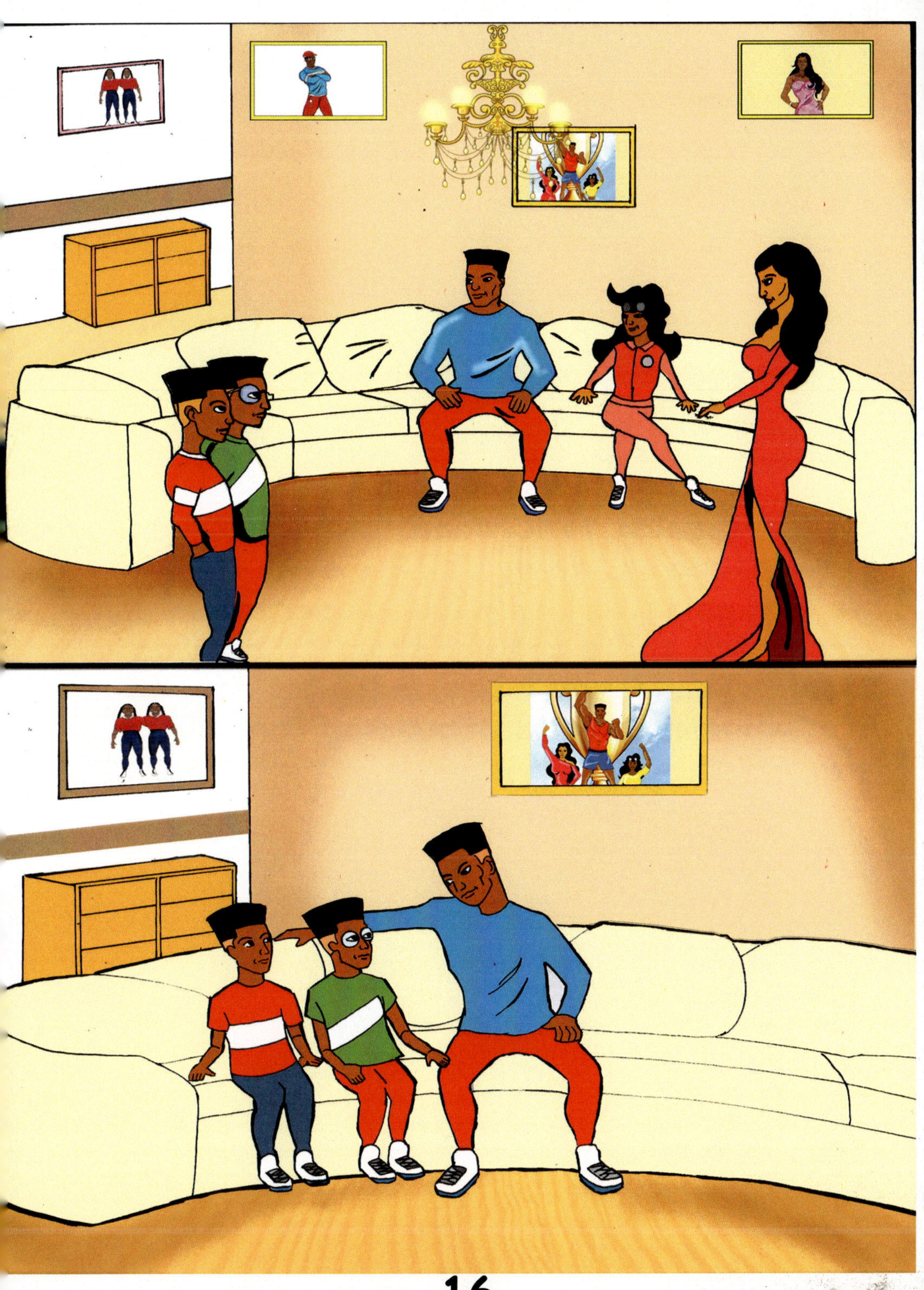

"We are going to 'Creams' the ice-cream parlor for ice-cream, then at 12 o'clock midnight, we are going to the Royal Observatory in Greenwich for a special show". This was strange, as I had been dreaming of a bright star shining over that building for the last two months.

Martin looked at me excitedly, 'it is going to be a special night', I heard him think, mum continued talking "the stars will be aligned in order and the Ankh Tutankhamun Artifact, 'The Key of Life', will be on display there". I thought to myself, this was a weird way of celebrating our 8th birthday. I did not want to go, however I knew I needed too.

Dad explained that, 'The Key of Life' artifact is only put on display, every eight years and only for eight hours. After which 'The Key of Life' is locked away for another eight years.

That evening, Dad gave each of us a black ninja outfit, I thought we were going to a dressing up party, oh how I was wrong.

We got on the train to Greenwich, I remember seeing the London eye, the Shard, Big Ben and the Cutty Sark. The stars were twinkling brightly; all the lights in the city were beaming beautifully like jewels on a crown.

We were walking past the Cutty Sark,
when Mum glanced at her watch,
just as it struck eleven forty-five,
we had fifteen minutes to get to the
Royal Observatory in Greenwich park,
for the show.

When we finally reached the main gates
to the park, they were locked.
My parents and Cleo all looked at each other,
then slowly they pulled down their ninja masks
over their faces, Martin and I did the same.

We all climbed over the gate, ninja style,
as I looked up to the night sky,
I saw this bright blue star shining.
The glow was so warm and inviting,
it felt like it was calling me to follow it.
We ran up the hill to The Royal Observatory,
as we approached the building
my parents stopped suddenly and turned to us.

“Can you feel anything” they asked, Martin nodded yes,so did I. They all, looked nervous, even Cleo,I asked them “what’s going on”.
The star, I had seen earlier that night, was brighter and now right over our heads, we all walked into the main room of the Observatory.
The light above us, had now become blinding.

Then we heard a voice "Tonight is one of the most magnificent nights in the Powerful family history. It is on this night the twins Marcus and Martin Powerful, will receive their powers, to help change the world for the better; you both are a part of the Powerful family bloodline, which is a great honour".

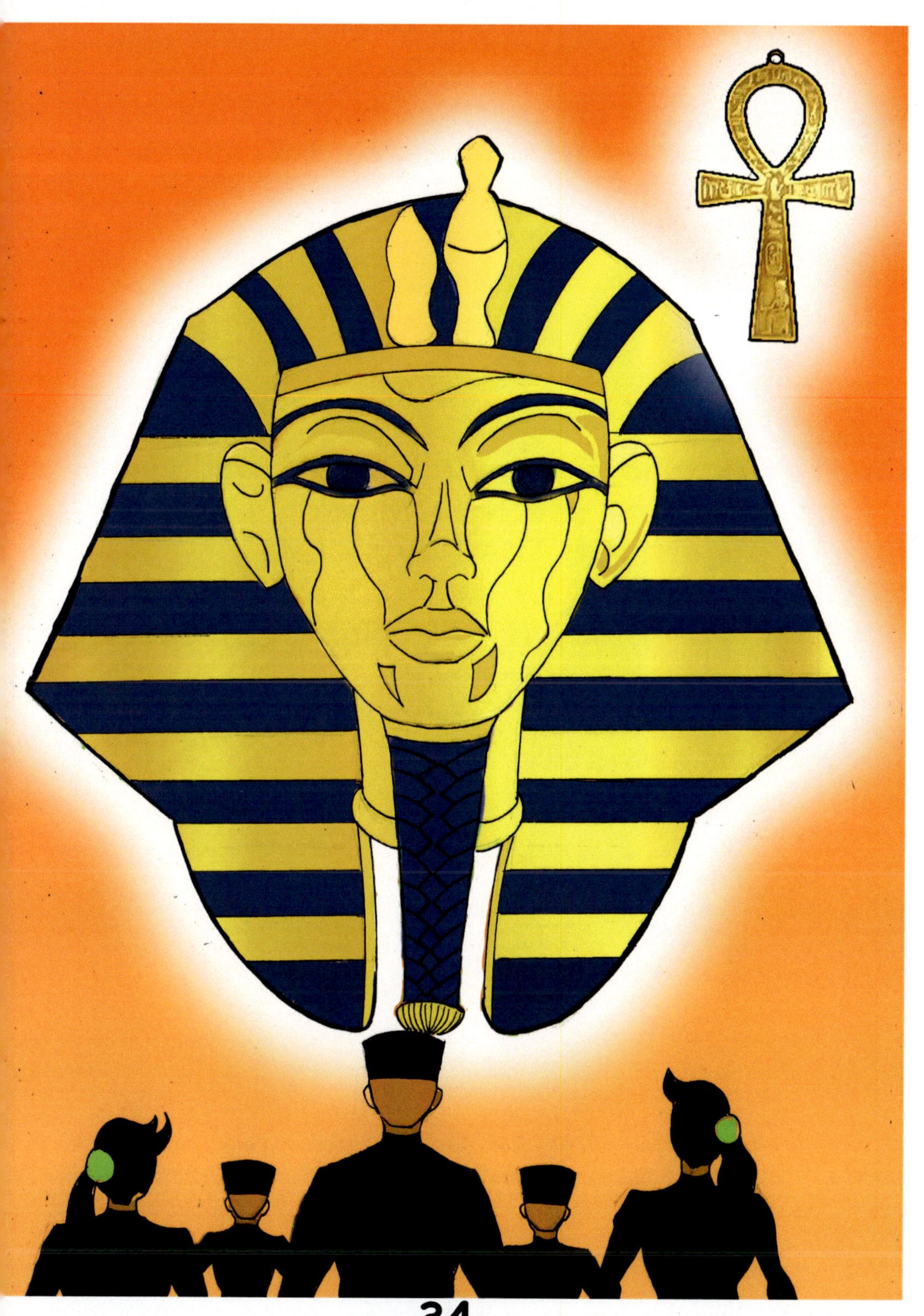

“We originate from Africa, Tutankhamun
was our king and it is through the
Ankh Artifact ‘The Key of Life’,
when touched, at midnight, on a Powerfuls
eighth birthday, it will unlock
that person’s power
and the Powerful family will all
receive new powers.

Martin looked at me,I looked at him,
this was crazy, why did this not feel strange or weird, deep down inside,
I thought my family was special but being super heroes, no way.The bright light began to change into a person.

The person of light moved towards 'The Key of Life' and touched it, the voice then spoke again "Marcus, Martin come forward and touch the Ankh artifact", we did as we were told. As I touched 'The Key of Life', I knew what my power was, I could hear other people's thoughts and Martin knew he could see into the future.

Our parents and Cleo came forward to touch the Ankh, the person of light nodded its head and spoke "You are all of a kind and clean heart, you too will receive your new powers". As soon as they touched 'The Key of Life', we all begun to float.

The bright light began to dim and the voice said "Welcome Marcus and Martin Powerful, make us proud and remember you can tell no one of your powers, it must remain a secret, to keep the family safe, Martin and I nodded yes, then the light disappeared

I cannot believe what just happened, did my family and I received the power of flight, what an amazing night. We all floated down to the ground. "Mum" I mumbled, who was that person of light that spoke to us". "That was our ancestors, contacting us from Africa to remind us that we are from the Powerful family bloodline and to inform us that only when we are kind to others and respectful, can we receive our powers" she replied.

I now know why the Powerful family are great at everything, we are a family of superhero's. Cleo my sister can heal someone with just one touch, my Mum can teleport and run faster than the speed of light, my Dad has super strength and can travel through time, my twin brother Martin can see the future and as for me, I can hear peoples thoughts.

I KNOW YOUR EVERY MOVE
DANGER AHEAD

This has been the best birthday of my life. I cannot wait to find out, what our first mission will be, to make the world a better place. Although, until then tonight we can go for a flight around London, to celebrate, Powerful family, love, peace and unity, whoosh